I Told You So!

The Adventures of
William and Thomas

I Told You So!

The Adventures of William and Thomas

Mark Gunning

Illustrated by Kathy Goodwin

Itchygooney Books

Text Copyright © 2019 Mark Gunning
Edited by Stephanie Sims

ISBN 978-0-9950670-6-6

Itchygooney Books
Niagara Falls, Ontario
www.itchygooneybooks.com

Dedicated to my kids, Taylor, Alex and Ty.

Acknowledgments: This book was made with the help of the following people. My wife Stephanie and my kids, who had to listen to my stories over and over, and who still do. To Stephanie Sims, my loyal editor. A big shout-out to Kathy Goodwin for her help with the illustrations. A special acknowledgment to Andy Thomson. A big thanks to my son Ty for helping with the ideas. Last but not least, to all my students from Peace Bridge past and present. Hope you enjoy!

Books by Mark Gunning

Available in Print and ebook

I Told You So!
      The Adventures of William and Thomas
I Told You So!
      The Journey Continues
I Told You So!
      Strike Three, You're Out!

Coming Soon

I Told You So!
      Back 4 More

www.itchygooneybooks.com

www.facebook.com/itchygooneybooks/

Table of Contents

Chapter 1

Harry and the Tree

My best friend William and I have a knack for getting into trouble. Sometimes it's not so much trouble, but more like things happen to us. You might say, trouble comes easy for us. William texted me to get to his house.

William

Today 9:23 AM

Tree ~ front yard!

What time?

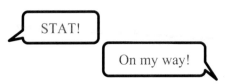

Now **STAT** has many different meanings. The number one meaning according to William was get to his house **ASAP**. I grabbed my bag of gear, which I'll explain later, and headed straight for the door.

It was a good thing that William only lived a couple houses over from me. I could get there in less than a minute. (By the way, did I mention that William was sometimes very impatient? Well, he was.)

William was standing on his lawn looking up at the biggest tree in his yard. Right at the very top of the tree was his model glider that he had built himself just the week before.

There was no way that William would leave his beloved glider without trying everything he could to get it down. The two of us decided to go to '**The SHOP**' to see what we could use. William quickly reached in his pocket and produced a set of plans. He had already drawn them up before I got to his house. William quickly put them up on the board above his workbench and studied them carefully. They looked fairly simple...

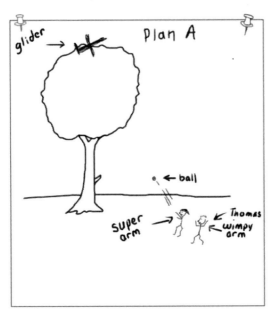

The first plan involved throwing my lucky baseball, which I carried in my backpack everywhere I went. It was autographed by my favourite Blue Jay of all time. I didn't want to use it, but William figured it was heavy enough to do the job. He pulled the plans off the board and the two of us headed to the tree and initiated the first plan.

I got first honours since it was my ball. I was happy that William was at least letting me go first. I opened my backpack and pulled out the ball and prepared myself. My first throw sailed into the tree and passed right through all the leaves and branches. I tried a few more attempts before William grabbed the ball from me and threw it as hard as he could. Well, that didn't work out so well! The ball ended up stuck in the branch right beside the glider. (At that moment I thought to myself, what a great idea William!) William scratched his head and then reached in his back pocket to produce the other plan.

Plan B was also simple. One of us would climb the tree and get the glider down safely. That is when William asked... sorry 'made' me climb the tree to retrieve it. I was a pretty good climber, but the glider and ball were stuck near the top of the tree. At this point I told him it wasn't a very good idea since the tree was very tall. Unfortunately, it didn't matter to William.

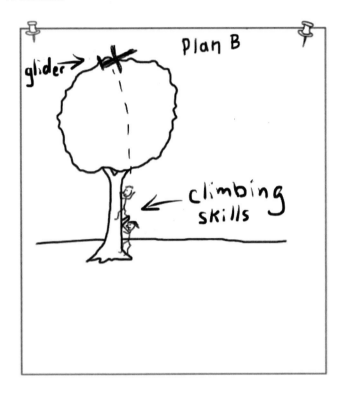

Things were going well as I was making my way up the tree when I couldn't go any further. I wasn't tall enough or strong enough to reach the next closest branch. Looking down I could see William was not very happy with my lack of progress. So, I slowly climbed back down and bet him he couldn't make it.

Around here, a bet was as good as a dare. It was an unwritten law with the kids in my neighbourhood. Once a dare or bet had been issued, it had to be done, or at least attempted. No questions asked. William spit in his hands, rubbed them together, and grabbed a hold of the tree.

This is the point in time that I'll mention that William outweighed me by about 60 pounds. Remember that for later on. I always say, better to be safe than sorry.

I know what you're thinking. How is the big boy going to make it up the tree? Surprisingly, William was a very good climber. He made it up to the first branch and then reached for the second branch pausing to get a better grip. I noticed that he was beginning to sweat pretty good. He continued to climb branch after branch and stopped to wipe his hands on his shirt. I'm not sure what the logic was when he spat on his hands before he began to climb, but then again, when did 'we' use logic?

The journey didn't last very much longer as William got stuck on the next branch. William had made it roughly more than halfway up the tree when things began to head south.

William's arms began to tire, and he was losing his grip. I stared straight up as William began to slowly fall. Then he finally let go. I remember closing my eyes and running from the base of the tree. (Hey, I didn't want to be the one to break his fall.)

I waited to hear the sound of William hitting the ground. Strangely, there wasn't one. So, I slowly opened my eyes looking up at where William was a moment earlier. I didn't see William, he was gone. Then I heard some grunting sounds and looked down near the base of the tree. There was William, hanging from a very tiny branch only a few feet off the ground being held up by just his belt. (Now that's what I call lucky!)

William began to wiggle to get unstuck. As he continued to squirm, he began to slowly turn upside down for what seemed like forever to me. This is the point in time that I just stood there staring, thinking of what to do next. William's face was beginning to turn bright red. I had to do something – but what?

Quickly, I jumped into action and began trying to twist William upright. It was no use. I wasn't strong enough. Just then the funniest thing happened. He slowly began to slide out of his pants.

I had to make another quick decision. Did I help him or take some pictures to post on our website? Quickly I proceeded to do the right thing. I grabbed my cell phone out of my backpack and snapped some pictures as fast as I could, making sure I had some really good ones to put on the site.

I know what you're thinking, why would you do this to your best friend? (Well, wouldn't you?)

I happen to have a funny (sometimes weird) sense of humour and when something extremely funny happens – I laugh – a lot. I began to giggle and laugh as he continued to hang upside down on the tree. By now, William was not very pleased with me and had had enough. Then he started to yell. I can't exactly remember what words he used. Okay I do, but I know I shouldn't write them down in case any adult ever sees this book.

With all the noise and everything going on, William's sheepdog Harry raced around from the backyard and stopped at the base of the tree and looked up. At the exact moment Harry stopped, William's butt popped out of his pants. William began to scream even louder.

Harry thought William was playing and began to pull on William's underwear. What was I to do? I took a few more photos for future use and ran to get his mom who was in the house. When I got to the front door I knocked and began laughing hysterically. William's mom opened the door and heard all the commotion going on. I couldn't even speak to her, but she knew something was wrong. However, she wasn't sure what to think. His mom spotted William hanging in the tree and ran out the front door. The neat thing was William had a pretty cool mom and she ran to the tree and began laughing as she scooted Harry away from William. Just as I was getting my laughter under control I began to laugh again. Tears were now running down my cheeks. There was William's mom and I both staring and laughing at William.

By now, William was not a happy-camper. He had definitely had enough of Harry and my laughing. To be honest – I wasn't sure what to do because I knew he would be mad – REALLY mad once he got down!

William's mom carefully got him unstuck and lowered him to the ground. His face was still beet red. I believe that's when I said, 'I told you so'. William looked at me and then looked at his mother, then at me, then his mother again. I started to snicker, trying to bite my lip. At that moment, William took one more look at both of us and then without warning, he came after me.

One good thing about being smaller was that I was fast. I turned and headed across his yard and climbed his grandparents' fence and headed for my house without ever stopping. Once I got to my house I turned around in my driveway and saw that William was still standing in his yard by the fence with a very annoyed look on his face. William just stood there and stared for a moment.

Suddenly, a huge gust of wind picked up and lifted the glider out of the tree. The glider gently landed at William's feet. Another gust picked up and this time my baseball fell out of the tree and landed right on top of his glider, crushing it.

William bent down and picked up his crushed glider. Now I thought that was funny. I busted out laughing again and that's when William snapped. I actually didn't think he would do anything since I was so far away, but then again you never knew what William would do when he was mad. William backed up a few steps and took a flying leap at his grandparents' fence, clearing it by what I would say was a new world record. He was coming my way and fast. As William got closer and closer, I thought it best to go inside where it was safer.

I ran to my front door and quickly opened it, slamming it shut behind me as I went in. Just to be safe I put on the double lock. My mom was standing in the kitchen looking at me. Without saying a word, I smiled and headed for my room. Just then I got a text from William.

William

Today 3:37 PM

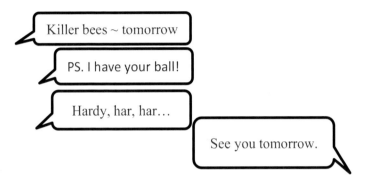

This meant only one thing. William had a new plan. I wondered what would happen tomorrow.

Oh, I almost forgot to tell you something from earlier. I brought my backpack everywhere with me and it always had some pretty cool stuff in it. I'd tell you more, but you'll just have to keep reading to see what else was in it.

Chapter 2

The Killer Bees

I heard a chime and realized it was a text from William. I grabbed my phone and looked.

William

Today 8:57 AM

Bring slingshot, 10 AM

The good thing about William was that he easily forgot about his mishaps and was ready for the next adventure. Earlier in the week, we heard his grandmother talking about a beehive along her driveway and that it was dangerous for the kids in the neighbourhood.

William had devised a plan to get rid of the bees and today was the day. I quickly ate and got ready to go over to his house. Around ten o'clock I grabbed my backpack and headed out the door. I took a quick detour over to his grandparents' house to investigate the beehive and assess the situation for myself.

Hanging from the tree was one of the biggest beehives I had ever seen. Once I had scoped out the hive, I headed straight for William's. I arrived at his house and quickly walked over to his garage, or what we called *THE SHOP*. There was William hunched over his workbench drawing up a new set of plans for today.

The plans were pretty cool looking. We would carefully get within shooting distance and take out the hive with a slingshot. Once the bees were angry, they would leave the hive and move on to somewhere else. William had even drawn up the escape route on his map so we would be able to get away unharmed. Everything looked foolproof.

We grabbed our gear and headed next door to his grandma's. William went first and I followed him as he snuck right up to the hive. It looked fairly quiet, so we paced ourselves a good distance from the hive. I set my backpack down and pulled out my slingshot. I would get to take the first shot. Carefully, I loaded it up, pulled back, aimed and fired. PFFFFFTT! I quickly fired off another shot and then another. Not being sure if I hit it, William yanked the slingshot out of my hands and fired before I even knew what was going on. PFFFFFTT! Direct hit!

Immediately there were a number of bees circling the hive. After a few more shots from William the bees were getting very agitated, but they weren't leaving. Things were not going as planned so we decided to head back to the shop to gear up for plan B.

Back in the shop William was looking closely at his next plan. This time it looked quite impressive. It involved the use of a toilet plunger, some bungee cords, a hammer and two old hockey sticks. This I thought was going to be good.

William also had devised an emergency outfit that he would wear to protect himself from the bees if things went right, or should I say wrong. One flaw in his emergency plans was the fact he only had one safety suit and not two. I didn't put any more thought into this. We quickly took two of his old road hockey sticks and sharpened the butt ends so we could push them into the ground. Then William grabbed a handful of bungee cords from his dad's tool chest and shoved them in my backpack.

He then sent me around to knock on his back door to distract his mother while he went inside to get a toilet plunger. His mom must have known we were up to something because she started to interrogate me. I tried to give my best answers, but soon I panicked and ran away. During this distraction, William somehow managed to sneak the plunger by her.

We were almost ready for the big moment when I suggested it wasn't such a good idea. I told William that we might get stung by the angry bees. William would have no part in listening to me and scurried back into his house. Patiently, I waited in his garage for him to return.

Ten minutes later William emerged wearing a bright orange pair of ski pants, matching ski jacket and a pair of steel-toed work boots that looked a little too big. He then found a pair of winter gloves and hacksaw in the garage and handed them to me. I stuffed them in the backpack and waited to see what he would do next.

The next part confused me as William grabbed his big red dirt bike helmet and proceeded to put it on. (More on that later.)

William and I carefully headed back over to his grandparents' house and began to set up. We decided that the shot must come from very close range. It was beginning to make more sense now as to why William was wearing all the extra clothing and helmet. However, I thought it was funny as William struggled to force the hockey sticks into the ground as the temperature began to soar.

After about fifteen minutes of setting up we had almost everything ready to go. The only thing left was to notch the end of the plunger and then let it fly. We accomplished this by carefully using a hacksaw to notch the end. By now William was beginning to get a bit too warm and I could tell, as beads of sweat ran down his face. We needed to take a practice shot so William aimed in the opposite direction and shot. The plunger sailed through the air and travelled about twenty feet. It looked like it was going to be a huge success.

I had to help William get his gloves on and then flip his visor down on his helmet. William turned and looked at me. It was funny how he reminded me of an astronaut from a really bad low budget movie.

Suddenly, that gave me an idea for another adventure. However, for now that idea would have to wait. In all the excitement, I forgot to get out my phone and record the future events. I know I'll regret not recording it because folks won't believe me when I tell them what happened next.

By now William's visor was starting to fog up and he was having difficulty seeing. William grabbed the plunger and placed it carefully on the bungees, lining up the notch and motioned me to get back. I quickly ran from the area and stood patiently watching to see what would happen next.

William pulled back with all his might and sat on the ground aiming the plunger at his target. He turned his head in my direction and gave me a nod.

The moment of truth had arrived. William steadied his aim and then let the plunger fly. It sailed through the air closing in on the hive. I closed my eyes and waited for the sound of a perfectly aimed shot. What happened next is hard to believe unless you were actually there to witness it.

I opened my eyes to see William still sitting on the ground with both hands on his helmet, shaking his head. I know you're not going to believe me, but the plunger was stuck to the side of the hive. The two of us just stared at the hive in disbelief. Finally, William jumped up and walked towards the hive and stopped when he got directly underneath it. The plunger was slowly swinging in the air along with the hive. Quickly, I began to think of how we could get the plunger off without getting stung when the beehive and plunger came crashing down on William.

The hive burst open when it hit William directly on the top of his helmet. As I stood and watched admiring William's work, William started to frantically jump up and down waving his arms. That's when I heard him start to scream. His visor was now fully fogged up and he began to run in circles as he had no idea where to go. He struggled to flip up his visor because of his clumsy gloves he had chosen and suddenly began to run in my direction. He continued to scream and wave his arms wildly in the air.

Once I realized that the bees were all around him attacking, I took off for my house in a mad dash. A streaking blur of orange caught the corner of my eye as William tore past me, arms still wailing in the air.

At this point I stopped and watched him go. He zigged to the right and suddenly took a sharp left and headed for his house at an incredible pace. He approached his grandparents' fence and instead of jumping it this time, William lowered his head and ran straight through it.

There was a tremendous crash as splintered fence boards flew through the air. I believe his helmet helped to destroy the fence on his way through or perhaps it was just his size. I'll never be certain for sure, but I do know who'd be fixing it. I'm sure his grandma was not going to be happy with him.

There were a few more loud screams from William before he dropped and rolled on the ground. By now his mother had heard the commotion outside and came running out to see what was going on.

As she ran out the front door William flew past her and disappeared into his house. That's when I decided it would be safer to head indoors, just in case the bees decided to seek revenge elsewhere. I set my backpack down by the front door and headed for my room. I thought it best to wait and let William contact me. As I lay on my bed, I couldn't help but think about what a nice shot William had made.

Chapter 3

Chili Anyone?

Roughly a week had passed since I last saw William after the killer bee incident. According to his mom, William had been stung thirty-seven times all over his body. The only place he didn't get stung was his face and head, thanks to his helmet. It was hard to tell he had been stung unless he took his shirt off and he wasn't too keen on doing that. William was trying to avoid me until all the spots had gone down in case I tried to take a picture of him. Unfortunately for him, I ran into his mother at the mailbox and she told me she had photos from the incident and that she would give me copies. (What a cool mom!) Perhaps these photos would come in handy for the future. I couldn't wait any longer, so I grabbed my phone and texted William and waited for a reply.

William

Today 9:35 AM

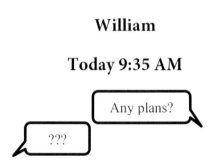

A couple minutes later he responded with:

Now I know what you're thinking, who is Granny Grunt? Granny Grunt was William's grandma from out of town. Let's just say she wasn't exactly the nicest person to meet. I grabbed my backpack and headed for

William's to see what his latest plan was. I arrived to find William standing in front of his workbench with a new set of plans on the board.

It turned out that William's parents were going out of town for a week and Granny Grunt was staying to watch William and his little brother Adam. The last time she stayed, William was grounded for a month and lost the use of his phone, video games, and any free time. More on that later.

William's plan was to get revenge on his granny by feeding Harry some leftover chili and then having Harry spend the night sleeping on his grandma's bed. William explained that his dad had made the chili and it was EXTRA spicy! You know what that would mean. Gas city! William then headed inside and was back in a few minutes with the leftover chili and Harry's bowl. He filled the bowl right to the top and plopped it on the ground with a thump!

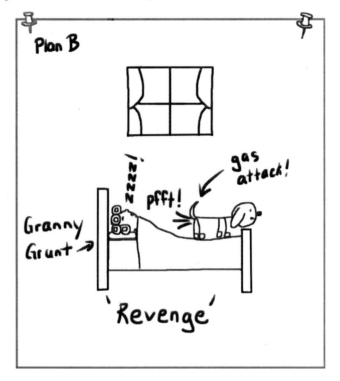

I then asked William if it was a good idea and he assured me that there was nothing to worry about this time. The only side effect would be lots and lots of gas. Harry must have heard the bowl because he appeared out of nowhere and gobbled down the entire contents in seconds flat. Harry hung out with us for a while in the garage. Moments passed when suddenly, Harry's stomach let out an enormous rumble and then as fast as he had appeared, he turned and was gone.

Thinking nothing of it, we headed inside to say goodbye to his parents and anxiously awaited the arrival of Granny Grunt.

A short time later, Granny Grunt arrived and gave us the customary grunt as William tried to be extra nice to her. Once she was settled in and his parents were on their way, we headed out back to play *MANHUNT*. This time it was William's turn to hide and I would try to locate him. As was customary with us, I gave him a five-minute head start to find the perfect hiding spot. Before he left, William put camouflage paint all over his face to make it more realistic, grabbed his Nerf rifle and with a warlike cry, howled and was gone. I sat down on one of his lawn chairs in the garage and opened my backpack. I quickly located my air-rifle and carefully loaded it with foam bullets and got ready to search for William.

William had a knack for hiding so that he was extremely difficult to find. I figured my best chance was to take my time and force him to blow his cover when he got bored of waiting for me. I wandered around for about half an hour and couldn't find any sign of William. I continued to scan the backyard and then thought maybe he headed towards his grandparents' house next door. I began looking in the bushes and around the yard when I noticed something out by his grandparents' old shed. I ran from tree to tree diving and flipping all the way there so I wouldn't be noticed. (I saw this on a TV show and figured if it worked for them, it might just work for me.)

As I got closer to the shed, I noticed something in front of it. I dropped to the ground and pulled out my binoculars from my backpack. Carefully, I scanned the area and focused in on what I thought was my target. Squatting in the grass was Harry. From what I could see, Harry was doing his business. It must have been the chili! Then I heard a horrible screeching voice coming from William's house. It was Granny Grunt calling or screaming (not too sure which) for Harry. Harry finished up and headed across the yard and back to William's house.

I continued to scour the area for William when I had an idea. I could climb the pile of logs behind the shed and get on the roof to have a better look for William. It'd be the perfect lookout spot!

I moved as quietly as I could and got onto the log pile. As I was climbing, I could hear a noise that sounded kinda like a bear. I froze in my tracks and listened closely. It took me a few moments to figure out the sound. Soon it became very familiar. The bear sound was only William snoring. I slowly peeked my head over the edge of the roof and saw William lying on his stomach near the front of the shed's roof with his Nerf gun in one hand. I figured he must have gotten tired of waiting for me and fell asleep. I quickly devised a plan to attack William by surprising him. We called this the element of surprise!

I slowly placed my rifle on the edge of the roof for support and steadied my aim. All I had to do now was yell really loud and he would jump up and I could take my shot.

Without hesitating I let out a piercing scream. Startled, William jumped to his feet with his rifle and swung around to face me. That's when I immediately fired my rifle.

In super slow-motion William grabbed his chest and dropped his gun as the foam bullet ricocheted off his body. It was a direct hit!

At this point it was clear to me by the look on his face that he had seen too many old war and western movies. He began to stagger backwards like they did in the movies. However, William was standing too close to the edge of the roof when he did this. In a split second, he was gone. Thud!

I climbed onto the roof and ran to the edge and peered over. There lying on the ground was William. At first, I thought he was dead. Then he began to move his arms and legs very slowly. He opened his eyes wide and looked straight up at me. He had a very weird expression on his face. Then he made his way to his feet and turned around. William had something stuck on his back. At that moment, I noticed that William had landed on something soft, brown, and squishy.

Yes, you guessed it. William had landed directly on the spot where Harry had been moments earlier. It didn't take William too long to figure out what was on his back. By the look on his face, he could smell it too. Before I could get my cell phone out to snap a great picture he was darting across the lawn and heading for home. I only managed to get a few long-distance shots of him running away. Instantly I realized he would be back soon and not very happy with me. Though he was the one to fall off the roof, he would blame me for what had happened. Quickly, I gathered my belongings and raced for my house. Sometimes it was best to let him cool down. The funny thing was, the chili was his idea.

Once I got to my house I went inside and headed to my room. To pass the time I began uploading the photos I had taken of William to the website so my friends would be able to see what had happened to William. As I was doing this, I realized that William was going to be extremely angry with me. After thinking briefly about taking them down, I decided to leave them on. They were pretty funny!

Later on, I received a text from William.

William

Today 11:15 AM

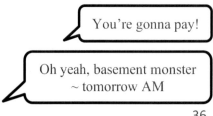

Seems he was over what happened earlier today. Or was he? It didn't matter, the monster text got my curiosity.

Chapter 4

The Basement Monster

I woke up to the sound of a text message and ignored it. It was early morning and I still wanted to enjoy a few more minutes of sleep. Ding! A moment of silence. Ding! Another one. This continued for a few more minutes. Finally, I reached for my phone on my nightstand and located it after a few attempts.

William

Today 7:52 AM

Get here ASAP!

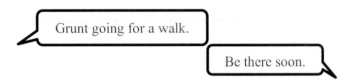

Grunt going for a walk.

Be there soon.

William wanted me to come to his house right away. His granny had just left the house to go for a walk and there was a small window of opportunity to pull off his next "so-called brilliant idea". I got dressed quickly, grabbed a quick bite to eat and headed over to William's. As I approached his house, I could hear a strange noise coming from his garage.

By now I had slowed down to a snail's pace and was confused by the odd sound. It sounded sort of like a cross between an angry bear and a crazed snake.

Maybe it was just William snoring again, but I had to find out. The sound suddenly stopped and changed to another strange sound. This time it sort of reminded me of a monster from one of the classic horror movies William and I had watched the summer before.

The noise suddenly stopped again and was followed by a very familiar sound ~ William laughing hysterically. I turned the corner and headed slowly into the garage to see William sitting on a chair by the workbench. His face was red, tears running down his cheeks. He was laughing to himself. Glancing towards the workbench I saw a new set of plans he had drawn up.

I wasn't sure what was going on, so I walked over and took a closer look. The plans showed William singing (or talking ~ I wasn't quite sure at that moment) into a microphone as part of Plan A, and the two of us (represented by some awesome stick figures I might add) blocking a door in Plan B. I stared at William for a moment with a confused look on my face and then he filled me in on the plans.

The plans were quite simple, William wanted to record monster noises into his tablet so he could send the sounds by Wi-Fi to the downstairs speakers in the playroom. This would make it appear that the noises were coming from the basement. These mysterious sounds would scare his little brother Adam.

Adam had gotten William into trouble the day before when he inadvertently told his granny that William had given Harry all the leftover chili in an attempt to seek revenge due to a previous grounding.

As part of his punishment, William had to clean up after Harry as he recuperated from all the spicy chili. As William explained, it was a little bit of payback for Adam telling on him.

William continued to explain his new plan with all the details. The gist of it was that the two of us would pretend not to hear the first sounds that would be coming from the basement. (Part of all our hard work.) After a while, I was to ask William if he heard something coming from the basement. William would then walk slowly towards the basement door and pause as a loud crash would occur downstairs, courtesy of the recording. I was then to creep over and stand behind William acting scared. The basement door would then be secretly opened just enough by William so he could look down through the crack and a rather loud roar would be heard, if timed just right. After the monster noise from the basement, it would be followed by the two of us screaming as loud as we could.

Hopefully, his little brother would be standing directly behind us for protection. His little brother Adam would be terrified! At this point in time I suggested to William that it wasn't such a good idea and that he might get grounded again. He proceeded to ignore me and went on to his plans.

We needed to finish the sound effects before Granny Grunt got back from her walk with his little brother or she would likely piece together what we were doing. The two of us decided to start the recording with some low-level noises and some rattling sounds. At this point William thought it would be perfect to continue recording silence for a bit before making some more noises. For the next half hour William and I hit garbage cans, rattled some tools and stomped around his garage as we continued to record. I must have gotten carried away because I grabbed one of his hockey sticks and whacked the side of his dad's garbage can a few times. (Leaving a massive dent ~ I might add.) However, something I would have to pay for later.

By now we were nearing final completion of the recording and figured we needed to add some additional sounds like someone, or SOMETHING was walking up the basement stairs. William put on his dad's work boots, yelled at me to bring the tablet and ran inside the house to finish the recording. William hurried to the bottom of the stairs as I began to record him stomping up the basement stairs. Once the two of us were happy with what we had accomplished, we hit the pause button and grabbed a quick drink in the kitchen.

By now we had pretty much everything recorded, but the final piece. The monster! William told me how he had been perfecting it whenever his granny took Adam for a walk. We ran back to the garage, closed the overhead door and set the tablet on the floor. I left the honours for William since this was his grand idea. I pulled up a stool and sat and watched the master at work.

William paced around the garage, took in a few deep breaths and scrunched up his face. Then he let out the most terrifying sound I had ever heard in my life! What came out of his mouth for the next sixty-eight seconds was what soon began to be known as ~ the **BEAR SNAKE!**

It completely caught me off guard as I fell backwards off the stool. William was so taken by the moment that he didn't even notice what had happened to me. I jumped up off the floor and sat back down. I found it truly amazing watching William as he continued the sound without ever pausing to take a breath. To this day I get chills down my spine when I think about the sound he made. He said it took a lot of skill. (I'd say ~ a lot of hot air!)

By now we were worried his granny and little brother would be returning soon, so we wrapped things up and went back inside to test the connection. Everything had to be PERFECT!

The tablet connected to the stereo system flawlessly. I adjusted the volume while William stood at the basement door listening closely. His dad had added a set of high-end speakers to the downstairs playroom which made it very convenient and realistic for us. After about twenty minutes of practicing we had our timing down pat. Now all we had to do was wait for nighttime to arrive. Just then, I received a text from my mom to come home for lunch. William and I quickly discussed a time and I disappeared out his front door and ran for my house. As I was running home, I noticed Granny Grunt and Adam walking up his driveway. That was cutting it close.

Meanwhile at my house, to kill time, I got on my computer and surfed the *Net*. Time was dragging by ever so slowly, so I decided to upload some more recent photos I had taken of William and posted them online. As I posted some of the photos, I thought about how mad William might get. Oh well, I thought to myself. He's a big boy and he'll get over it.

Eventually, my mom called me for supper and I quickly scarfed it down. By now I could hardly wait for the big moment. As soon as it got dark, I was to head over to William's house so we could start the movie. The daylight began to fade, and I put on my shoes, said good-bye to my parents, and headed over to William's. Granny Grunt greeted me at the front door.

I could tell by the look on her face that she wasn't too thrilled I was coming over that late. She hollered in her customary gruff voice for William to come to the door. Once he arrived, she looked the two of us up and down, grunted and headed up the stairs to her bedroom where she would reside for the evening. Harry followed her upstairs and was gone too. Our plan was going perfectly.

I walked into the family room and there sitting on the middle of the couch was Adam. He was patiently waiting for the movie to start. He loved watching movies with us and always enjoyed sitting right between us. I think it made him feel safe. (Poor little guy I thought to myself.) If he only knew what was about to happen.

As I got the movie ready, William hustled into the kitchen and made some popcorn. Whenever it was movie night, there was always popcorn. He also wanted to make sure that his granny was staying upstairs so he crept upstairs to make sure she was in her room.

A few minutes later William emerged from the kitchen with a gigantic bowl of popcorn. As the movie began, the three of us sat on the couch next to one another and stuffed our faces with popcorn.

William had chosen a classic movie based on one of my favourite cartoons. It was also a movie that wouldn't be too scary for Adam. Of course, that would all change later on.

William and I were really getting into the movie and almost forgot about our plan. We finally ran out of popcorn and realized that we had to start things soon. The movie had about half an hour to go when William decided to start the recording. It was time for us to put on a show. William carefully reached over the side of the couch and started the sounds playing on his tablet. It was now hooked into the wireless system and all we had to do was wait.

As the movie continued, I could begin to hear the strange noises coming from the speakers in the basement. William and I secretly glanced at each other so Adam wouldn't notice and smirked. It didn't take long for Adam to notice the sounds as well.

He began to look up and stared towards the basement door, then paused and went back to watching the movie. This continued on and off for the next few minutes and then there was a loud crash.

Adam was now inching closer and closer to my side and then slid right next to me. The look on his face said it all. This was my time to ask William if he heard any noises from the basement. William acknowledged that he too had heard something and paused the movie. Carefully, he crept towards the basement door. There was a loud thud! Then there was another loud noise.

He slowly motioned me over to the door and I snuck up behind him. By now, Adam had a very concerned look on his face. Slowly, William opened the basement door just a crack and peeked downstairs. It couldn't have been timed more perfectly as the monster sound roared from the basement speakers.

William turned and shouted at me to help. Just like we had thought, Adam had followed us to the door. He was now positioned behind me and he grabbed a hold of my leg, cutting off the circulation.

William slammed the door shut and leaned his shoulder into it. I reached around him and pushed on the door as well. Pounding footsteps could be heard coming up the stairs. The two of us screamed and hollered as we tried to brace the door. During all the commotion of the two of us hooting and hollering, William had carefully slipped his foot a few centimetres from the base of the door. Suddenly there was a huge thud against the door.

William secretly kept his foot against the door as he pulled on the door handle with one hand. This gave the appearance of something or someone trying to get out of the basement. The door appeared to open ever so slowly as I pushed, and William pulled. Adam screamed and continued to squeeze my leg even tighter. The monster was thumping on the door. With everything going on, everyone yelling and the **Bear Snake** roaring in the basement, William took his free hand and grabbed the side of his face to make it appear as if it was coming from behind the door.

At first, even I was convinced that something was coming out of the basement and I pushed the door closed. Just as it slammed shut the lights came on in the family room and Granny Grunt was standing there staring at us. She began hollering and the three of us spun around to see her standing there with green makeup and other stuff all over her face. She looked hideous! Actually, terrified for a moment, William and I screamed, opened the door and ran down the stairs. We left poor little Adam standing there with his granny.

We stayed in the basement for a few minutes and then decided it was time to face Granny Grunt. She did not look very happy at all. I was immediately told to head straight home and not to come back until she was heading back up North.

As for William, he had to sleep with his little brother Adam for two whole months after the incident. Adam had been experiencing very bad nightmares and his parents and granny felt it was an appropriate consequence for William's actions. Funny thing was, Adam turned out to be a chronic bed wetter. Go figure.

Chapter 5

The Ramp

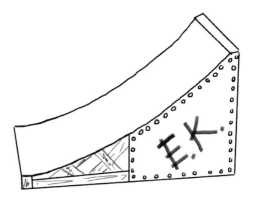

It had been five long days of being exiled from William's house until his grandma headed back up North. During this time, William had come up with a number of ideas on what we could do next for fun. Almost every thirty minutes, William texted me a new idea only to come up with another one shortly afterward. Unfortunately, William had to stay close to his house and was never really let out of his granny's sight while she remained there. (Well, could you blame her?)

Once William's parents were back home, and his granny had finally left to head up north my phone chimed and there was a new message from William.

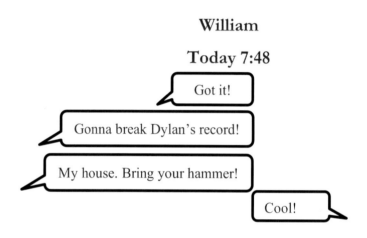

William

Today 7:48

Got it!

Gonna break Dylan's record!

My house. Bring your hammer!

Cool!

Dylan, you see, was the oldest kid in the neighbourhood and we all looked up to him. He was the coolest guy you could ever meet. However, my mother would disagree with that. Unfortunately, Dylan had gone away to college last fall and it just wasn't the same in our neighbourhood. (Yet my mom said it was much safer for all the neighbours.)

We learned so many cool things from Dylan, like how to drive a dirt bike, shoot a bow and arrow, and play guitar. I still remember seeing William cry as Dylan drove off in his car heading to college.

William still denies he was crying that day and claims he was trying to rub an eyelash out of his eye. Only problem was, William had burned off all his eyelashes a week earlier during a barbeque stunt gone wrong and didn't have any eyelashes at that time. (William made me swear to secrecy that I would never tell anyone what happened with the barbeque that day. However, he didn't say I couldn't write about it.)

In our neighbourhood we had a running total of personal records that had been set. Dylan was the recipient of the most records. For instance, Dylan had managed to eat twenty-seven hotdogs in five minutes, without throwing up! (Like I said, he was the coolest.)

Anyways, William was bound and determined to break all of Dylan's records as a tribute to the man himself. During his time spent (held hostage) in his room (Remember the Bear Snake?), William studied the Itchygooney Wall of Fame website we had created a few years earlier to showcase all our amazing stunts and records.

```
┌─────────────────────────────────────────┐
│         Itchygooney Wall of Fame!         │
│                                           │
│  Most hotdogs eaten at once               │
│          27 – Dylan                       │
│  Longest bike jump                        │
│          9 kids - Dylan                   │
│  Longest grounding                        │
│          3 months – Dylan                 │
│  Lamest excuse                            │
│          The baby did it! - William       │
│                                           │
└─────────────────────────────────────────┘
```

After viewing them very carefully, William had decided that today was the day he would build a monster ramp to break Dylan's bike jump of nine kids. Saturday would be exactly eight years ago to the day that Dylan had cleared nine of his friends lying down side by side with his bike.

The two of us were only toddlers at the time and had to listen to stories of how that day went down and how Dylan magically flew through the air. William had tried many different times to break Dylan's record only to have problems with his bike, the ramp, and his mom. He finally decided that he was ready to not only break the record, but CRUSH it!

Another text arrived. This time it said:

Today 7:50 AM

> Bring some duct tape too!

I ran to my garage, grabbed my dad's hammer and a roll of duct tape (my dad says it's the greatest invention ever) and rode my bike to William's. Upon arriving William was hunched over his workbench staring at his latest designs. The first design was pretty cool. On the first plan, it showed William flying through the air on his bike with his cape flowing in the wind. Below William were twelve kids lying on the ground. He looked truly amazing as he flew overhead.

William then asked me for my laptop, which I pulled out of my backpack, and quickly found a website that showed how to build awesome ramps. After a brief search, William had found the ramp that he said would help him smash the record. It was massive!

I then quickly looked at the second plan showing William holding the trophy for the longest bike jump ever.

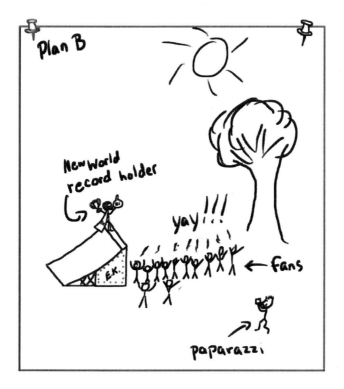

I then focused back on the plans on-line and asked him if he thought it was too big. Shaking his head at me, William clicked print and ran into his house to get a copy of the plans. Within minutes the two of us were carrying wood from his dad's shop from out back. Carefully we piled the wood on his driveway, laying the pieces out according to the plans. It looked like we would be short, so we grabbed his dad's riding mower and trailer and headed to my house to gather up the rest of the wood. The great thing about my dad was that he usually had whatever you wanted in his shop. He was kind of like a king pack rat. If you needed something, he usually had it.

It took us a while, but we eventually found all the materials to build the ramp. The ramp was going to be huge. When completed, it would be eight feet high and almost twenty feet long. His mother came out of the house at one point, took a look at the ramp, shook her head and walked back inside without saying a word. It looked like we would have no trouble from here on.

Roughly six hours later we had completed the ramp. Once the ramp was finished, William and I tried to move it. The ramp was extremely heavy due to all the two-by-fours we had used. We quickly decided it would have to stay facing the way it was. There was only one problem with where we had built the ramp, it was positioned right at the edge of where his driveway met the lawn. William would be able to pedal down his driveway and make his landing on the grass. This actually didn't seem so bad. Perhaps luck was finally on his side.

The two of us stood and admired our craftsmanship. It was a work of art! (I guess watching all those home renovation shows was paying off.) I grabbed my camera and took some photos of the ramp. This definitely was going to be added to the Itchygooney website.

William then ran to his garage, put on his helmet and wheeled out his bike. I moved back from the ramp and watched as William hopped on his bike and began to ride around the ramp in a giant circle. Quickly, he picked up speed and continued to circle around it. Then he tore off down the driveway heading towards the river. He skidded to a halt and waved at me. He stood staring at the ramp, his bike balancing between his legs. Then he placed his right foot on one pedal, pushed off and headed towards me.

The closer he got, the faster he went. William hit the base of the ramp and locked up the tires. I expected him to slide right off the top of the ramp and crash to the ground below. Screeching, his bike slid and stopped at the very top of the ramp with a few inches to spare. Now that was cool!

William smiled at me and then spun his bike around and coasted back down the ramp. He rode over to his garage, hopped off his bike and plopped himself on the stool in front of the workbench. Quickly, I ran over to see what he was up to.

Scribbled down on a piece of paper were the names of all the kids from our neighbourhood. Now we would just have to get them to be a part of local history. William explained to me again that Dylan had the record of jumping over nine kids and that to make the new record stand forever, he would need to surpass that number by not just one, but three!

Since it was mid-July, we figured we wouldn't have any trouble gathering up the necessary people to complete the stunt. Our first step was to coordinate the day and time for the big event. At the same moment, William and I had a fantastic plan to make up flyers to post around the neighbourhood. (William also wanted an audience to witness the historic event.) Together, we made a rough design of the flyer on paper. I then volunteered to create a good copy on my laptop and got to work right away. The flyer looked like this:

Historical Itchygooney Record
Breaking
Ramp Jump

Performed by William

Day: Saturday

Time: 12 Noon

Price: Free

As I worked on the flyer, William tore the list in half and placed my piece beside my laptop and then disappeared inside his house.

As soon as I was finished, I printed off a dozen copies and then began to text the people on my list. It took me approximately fifteen minutes to send out all the texts requests. Surprisingly, five of the six people responded back immediately saying they would be honoured to take part in the event. Just then William entered through the side door of his garage wearing a Superman cape that he had worn only a few Halloweens before. He thought it would make the event more memorable as he flew through the air. Adding to that, he said his dad used to tell him stories about the great *Evel Knievel* and that someday he would follow in his footsteps. (I'm not sure what he meant by that at the time.)

Eventually, William got around to his list and texted everyone. Then we got on our bikes and headed around the neighbourhood putting up the flyers where we thought they would get the most visibility.

With Saturday being only three days away, William felt that he needed some trial runs. However, instead of using the big ramp he chose to build a much smaller one to practice on. Back to work we went as we used the leftover wood to build a much smaller version of '**THE BEAST**'.

This time it only took us two and a half hours to build the scaled down version. Once we dragged the ramp in place William was back on his bike and started to practice jumping off of it. Everything was going smoothly. He landed each jump safely and felt more confident after each jump. To help judge the distance, I placed some beach towels down on the ground to represent our friends that he would try to clear. It looked like nothing was going to get in the way of a record setting accomplishment.

Over the next few days William continued to practice as I received verification from all twelve volunteers that they would be there Saturday. Soon, word got out and William had quite a large group of the younger neighbourhood kids watching him practice. He loved the attention so much that he started signing autographs at the end of each day. He even thought of building a booth and charging money.

I was left in charge of choosing the order in which people would be lined up on the ground. To make it fair, I invited everyone over that was to partake in the jump to witness the drawing of names that would make up the order. I wrote down all twelve names and placed them in a hat. William's little brother Adam came out to see what was going on and was allowed to pick the names.

One by one the names were drawn. The order of names would make up the line of kids starting at the base of the ramp, extending out to the end of the jumping area.

During the early selections, people were laughing and talking away like it was no big deal. That soon changed as the draw got down to the final five people. You could tell they were getting extremely nervous and did not want to be the final ones at the end of the line.

Eventually, the order had been selected and a few tears were shed. The unlucky ones drawn to be at the end of the line weren't laughing or smiling as they left to go home. Soon the talk of the neighbourhood was just how far could William jump? It was getting tense.

The next day I arrived at William's house to find him making some minor adjustments to his bike. After, he carefully checked the air in his tires to make sure they were at optimum pressure.

Normally, William was a pretty laid-back kind of guy, but today he had quite a serious look on his face. He decided he only wanted to make a few practice jumps, so I took a tape measure from his dad's workbench and headed over to the practice ramp. Upon measuring his last few attempts, it appeared he was only jumping far enough to get safely over four people. Would this be enough? Guess we'd have to wait and find out. (Glad I wasn't one of the few in line.)

Carefully, we went over his plans again and made some calculations, taking into account the height of the bigger ramp. William had it figured out that he would have just enough room to spare. (He told me that his teacher had taught his class about angles and that he did okay on the unit.) There was nothing to worry about. (As usual!) I headed back home and awaited the big day. I found it very hard to sleep that night. Was William really going to break the record?

Saturday morning finally came, and I hopped out of bed and got dressed as fast as I could. Quickly, I gulped down my breakfast, said goodbye to my mom and dad and went out the door. I was so excited that I forgot to bring my backpack. Realizing what I had done, I did a quick U-turn, flew inside the door, grabbed my backpack and was gone in a flash.

Within a minute, I was at William's house and hurried around the corner to his garage. Sitting on his bike at the bottom of the ramp was William. I let out a yell and ran over to him. He smiled and got off his bike. Without saying a word, he slowly walked up the ramp and stood at the top starring down towards the ground. I ran up beside him and looked down too.

Boy, did it ever look high from where the two of us stood. Then he sat down on the edge with his legs dangling from the side. Following suit, I carefully sat down beside him and waited for William to speak. He let out a huge sigh and then began going over all the details of the jump. He wanted me to check my camera to make sure it was charged and that I had enough room on the memory card to capture the moment. He did not want this historic moment to be lost forever.

By now it was ten o'clock in the morning and kids from all around were starting to show up. To keep William happy, I tested my camera and showed him the battery level was fully charged. It didn't take long for all of the willing participants to show up. I had my doubts that they'd all show up, but amazingly they all did. We climbed down off the ramp and I quickly went over the lineup that we drew and checked to make sure no one was getting cold feet.

While this was going on, William went back in his garage tweaking stuff on his bike. I glanced over to see him fidgeting with his brakes, yet I knew they were fine. He must have been extremely nervous and needed something to preoccupy his thoughts.

As it got closer to noon the crowd grew larger and was starting to make quite a bit of noise. William's mother came out of the house and went into the garage where William sat. After explaining things to her, he quickly reassured her that everything was going to be fine and gave her a big hug. Quietly she went back inside (not really knowing what was about to happen) as William worked his way to the opening of the garage and waved to the crowd. Everyone noticed him and cheered wildly. Then he spun around, walked to the workbench and pushed the button on his remote to close the garage door. The door then quickly shut, and he was gone.

At that time, it was quarter to twelve and I motioned his assistants to take their places by the ramp. For extra safety, many of the kids brought their bike helmets just in case William didn't succeed. I thought they were smart to do that, especially the few at the very end of the line.

Almost fifteen minutes had passed when there came a loud noise from inside the garage. It was music blaring like you had never heard before. It took me a second or two to realize that it was the theme song to a boxing movie I had seen with my dad. Then the garage door opened, as smoke began to pour out from inside. (I told you William was dramatic.)

Escaping from the cloud of smoke was William pedalling as fast as he could. He was wearing a white t-shirt with what appeared to be the initials E. K. duct taped to the front of his shirt. For safety, he chose to wear his dirt bike helmet that had saved his face from the devastation of the bees just a few weeks earlier. Flowing in the wind was his Superman cape. He looked awesome!

With a quick look at the crowd, he wheeled around near the ramp and then sped away down his driveway and came to a screeching halt. He got off his bike, waved to the crowd, flipped his visor down and jumped back on his bike.

It was now one minute to noon and the crowd became silent. I checked to make sure everyone was in their positions and then turned on my camera and got into place. I waved to William and gave him a thumbs up to let him know everything was a go.

Without hesitating, William began to pedal towards the ramp. He accelerated as he got closer and closer, pumping faster and faster as his bike approached the jump. He hit the ramp going at top speed and pulled back on his handlebars as his bike propelled off the top of the ramp. The crowd roared as William exploded off the ramp.

It was like time stood still as he floated through the air, his cape waving dramatically behind him. Somehow William even managed to pull off a complete **TAIL WHIP** to the delight of the crowd.

Everything that we had talked about was perfect, except for one thing. Due to his tremendous speed at takeoff, William propelled much further than planned and as he was coming out of the spin, he crashed into an overhead tree branch. The entire crowd froze as William collided with the tree and his bike came crashing to the ground.

Luckily, the bike cleared everyone laying on the ground below. Now I know you're wondering what happened to William. Right?

Let's just say he was lucky and not so lucky at the same time. Somehow William managed to get stuck on the tree branch and hung dangling roughly twenty feet in the air. (Sound familiar?)

I set my camera down (after taking a few good pictures) and ran to get his mom. His mom came running out and discovered what had happened. By now William was in a lot of pain and he was beginning to make some strange noises. I passed her my cellphone and immediately she called 911.

The ambulance and fire department arrived shortly to get William out of the tree. His mom had a concerned look on her face as William was loaded into the back of the ambulance.

I ran over to see how he was just before the paramedics closed the doors. Lying on the stretcher, William had a tremendous grin from ear to ear. I couldn't believe my eyes. He quickly told me how he had a possible fractured bone in his left arm and a broken collar bone to go with it as the doors to the ambulance slammed shut. He was so happy that he was just like his hero, E. K.

His mom then asked everyone to go home and got in her car to follow the ambulance to the hospital. I decided to pack things up and headed back to my house.

As for the record, after viewing the video with my family (at least twenty times), his bike had cleared the line of twelve kids and William had also cleared them too. It was official ~ William was now the new record holder of the longest bike jump in our neighbourhood. Congratulations had to go out to William! This was going up on the Itchygooney Wall of Fame website. (Oh yeah, I also had some nice photos of William hanging from the tree to add to it as well!

Chapter 6

Slip Slidin' Away

It was two weeks later, and William was slowly recovering from the ramp incident and was eager to get back into the swing of things. He texted me to come over and meet in the *'SHOP'*.

William

Today 9:15 AM

Shop.

On my way.

As always, I grabbed my backpack and made a beeline to William's. We sat down by his workbench and looked over all of the ideas he had written down while recuperating from the broken bones. Part of the list looked like this:

Joy Buzzer

Catapult

Ketchup Trick

Giant Kite

Fake Snow

Potatoes

Stunt Movie

We went over things a few times until William decided on the fake snow idea. William scribbled down his plans on a couple pieces of paper and explained how it would go down. Plan A involved us pulling dish detergent up to his room on the second floor.

A few years earlier his dad had entered a contest to create a slogan for dish detergent and won the grand prize ~ a life-time supply of dish washing detergent. Stacked along the wall in his garage were boxes and boxes of detergent. At first, his dad was very happy about winning until a new box arrived every month. That explained why they were piling up in the garage.

Even after giving some away, his dad still had too much. Upon hearing his dad complain, William had an idea to get rid of some of the soap and make his dad extremely happy.

The second part of the plan involved the two of us climbing out the window of his upstairs bedroom and sprinkling the soap down from the roof in front of the family room window of his house to make it look like it was snowing.

Since it was summertime, it would be really funny to see his dad's face once he noticed it coming down. I suggested that maybe a better idea was to load the boxes on his wagon and go door to door selling it. That way his dad would still be happy, and we'd make some money.

To get the soap into his room without getting caught by his mom, we decided to use a rope and bucket to haul it up. I shoved the rope under my shirt while William hid the bucket under his. Then we walked right through his family room and up the stairs to start our next plan. His mother gave us a strange look as we walked by like nothing was abnormal. I stayed in his room while he went back to the garage and loaded the soap onto his wagon and pulled it around to the front of the house.

As quietly as possible, William loaded one box at a time into the bucket and I hauled it up onto the roof. The roof had a nice overhang of roughly twelve feet which allowed us to set the boxes down for easy access and storage. Once we had enough boxes on the roof, William came inside and climbed out the window to join me.

Apparently, his dad was laying on the couch watching a baseball game and would notice the 'snow' as it came down. If all went as planned, he would come out the front door and William would yell – 'SURPRISE!' from the roof and I would take a picture of his dad's astonished look!

We opened the boxes and started sprinkling the soap from the roof. This continued for a number of minutes. Perhaps his dad wasn't paying attention, or he was really enjoying the game. So, we continued to dump the soap. While we were doing this, the sky suddenly darkened and out of nowhere it began to pour. William thought for a second and then stomped his feet on the roof and continued to pour the soap. Not even a minute later, his dad opened the front door and ran out to see where the 'snow' and noises were coming from. The water mixed with the soap made the front porch extremely slippery.

Let's just say, his dad skidded for a few feet before his legs went out from under him and he flew off the front porch and crashed to the ground. William yelled 'Surprise!' a bit too late as his dad rolled on the ground in extreme pain. During all the excitement I managed to get a few pictures of the big event. I'm sure I had a great shot of his dad's face as he spun around and fell onto the sidewalk.

It wasn't long before the ambulance arrived to take his dad to the hospital. The same paramedic (who we got to know as Paramedic Mike) who helped William two weeks earlier made a comment about frequent flyer miles to his dad. William's dad was not happy, as expected.

In the end, William's dad had broken his wrist while trying to prevent his fall. During his dad's unwanted 'time off' work, William had to do anything that his dad requested until he was able to go back to work. William's first job – clean up the soap!

WILL GRANNY GRUNT

BE BACK?

Glossary

ASAP is generally an abbreviation for, "As soon as possible"

BEAR SNAKE sound invented by William that sounds like a bear and a crazy snake combined

MANHUNT game that William, Thomas and sometimes their friends played in the backyard

Evel Knievel (E. K.) an American daredevil who was an icon of the 1970s

Net short for the Internet

STAT an abbreviation for "immediately"

Tail Whip kicking the bike while holding the handlebars so that the frame makes a 360 degree rotation while the rider does not rotate

THE SHOP place where the boys designed most of their plans

About the Author and Illustrator

Mark Gunning grew up in Chippawa, Ontario where he spent most of his youth playing outside with his friends. They had many fun adventures together and this has helped create some of the stories you have enjoyed today.

A teacher with the DSBN, Mark started his idea of writing children's books back in 2010 to share some of his stories with his students and getting them into writing. He and his wife Stephanie, have three children, a dog named Chewie, two cats and a budgie.

Kathy Goodwin is trying to perfect the art of drawing stick people, and often wonders why Mark decided to let her draw the pictures for his amazing books.

GOT A PLAN?

LET'S TALK

MARK GUNNING

Which character would you say you are more alike, William or Thomas?

I'd have to say I'm a little like William and a little like Thomas. Likely more Thomas than William. Or at least that's what I tell my mom.

Did you actually do any of the things you write about?

Unfortunately for my neighbours and parents growing up, yes I did do some of the things that I mentioned. But I had an accomplice. Without him I doubt I would have finished this book.

When did you decide to become a writer?

It was back in the late 90s when I read a book called *Captain Underpants* by Dav Pilkey. I was teaching and all the kids in the class were reading this book. I got myself a copy and after finishing it, I decided I would tell my own stories. Unfortunately, at that time I was just starting a family and had to put things on hold. It wasn't until around 2010 when I happened to meet a fantastic Canadian author doing an author visit at my school. After talking to him, I was motivated to start writing again and I finished my stories and then put them away.

What did you do as a kid?

I was lucky to have grown up in a unique part of Niagara Falls. My family owned a farm and so I got to experience different jobs and chores that helped me learn a number of life skills that a lot of kids don't experience these days. These experiences have helped me in my stories. I'm sure some of these events will transfer onto paper one of these days.

Based on your characters in your books, were you a big fan of school?

Hmmm. Do I have to answer that? I did enjoy school, but it was usually during gym time and recess. I do remember visiting the principal's office a few times. Oh, wait, am I off topic?

Did you really have friends named William and Thomas?

No, I didn't. I did have a best friend Mark. However, an interesting fact is my middle names are William and Thomas. Coincidence?

Growing up did you have any hobbies?

As a kid I collected hockey cards and stamps. However, most of the time I was outside playing sports like hockey, baseball, or football. I loved playing road hockey and was always in net most of the time. I also played with my action figures. Yes, they were action figures, not dolls.

Do you have plans for other kinds of books or series?

I have been thinking of writing a mystery series that would have William and Thomas solving mysteries. I loved watching *Scooby-Doo* cartoons when I was a kid and have always loved mysteries. I also have plans to write a more serious book that I say is for adults. I've started it, I just need to find the time to finish it.

What's your favourite movie?

That's a hard question to answer. I'd say I have more than just one favourite movie. I really enjoyed the *Star Wars* movies growing up. *The Lord of the Rings* series is also on my list. I also can't forget *Saving Private Ryan*. Come to think of it, my list goes on and on. Maybe I'll write a book on my favourite movies.

Do you have a sense of humour?

Yes, of course I do. If I had to describe it, I'd say I have a Canadian sense of humour eh.

Speaking of favourite movies, what is your favourite book?

Easy. *The Hobbit*. Read it back in high school and almost lost my mind when it became a movie.

Do you have kids of your own and if so, what do they think of you being an author?

To be honest, my kids just think of me as their dad. I don't think they really look at me as an author. Maybe I should ask them. Hey, Ty?

What do your parents think of your books?

I think that they're super proud and a bit shocked at some of the other stories that I tell them. I have so many other stories that I guess wouldn't make it into my books.

Where do you write your books?

I write them at home on my laptop. Sometimes I write them when I'm outside relaxing. When I do write, I need to have some music playing.

What type of music do you like?

I LOVE 80s rock, such as AC/DC and Def Leppard. So many great bands from that time period.

Did you have any other dreams growing up besides being an author?

My first dream was to be a professional hockey player or baseball player. Then I switched that to being a vet. A few years later I changed my mind and wanted to be a police officer and then a teacher. Finally, a few years ago I decided I wanted to be a children's author. It worked!

What would be your ideal dream job?

Being a Rockstar! Or an author!

Do you still play hockey?

Unfortunately, my body doesn't want me to play anymore. I really miss playing in net, but the days after I play just aren't worth it anymore. I say this to everyone, enjoy it while it lasts.

Have you had many jobs before this?

Oh my gosh. Let me think about that. Here, I'll write them down. My jobs included: a farm labourer, lawn cutter, house painter, Cutco sales rep, Rainbow sales rep, deli clerk, dishwasher, bakeshop employee, greenhouse worker, supply teacher, woodworker, teacher, and author. I think that covers it.

Do you have a favourite word?

I'd say my favourite word is shenanigans. I hope I spelled it right.

What do you do for fun?

I like to go golfing, fishing, and bowling. I just wish I had more free time to do other things.

Will there be a day when you decide to stop writing?

No way, I'll keep writing until I can't see the words on the page. Hopefully for a long time.

What is your favourite sport?

Being Canadian, I'd have to say hockey. Baseball is second. Football is right up there.

Do any of your kids play sports?

Currently, my son plays baseball and I help coach his team. It's very satisfying seeing him play and the other kids improve as they get older.

What is your favourite thing about being an author?

My favourite thing about being an author is when I do author appearances and meet the kids and their parents. I did a book club visit and had a fantastic time interacting with the kids. I love when they ask questions. I'm hoping that one day I will travel the world promoting my books and talking with kids. I think reading and writing is so important.

What is your favourite story in your book?

My favourite story is *The Killer Bees*. Most of that story is true. You'll have to figure out what isn't.

What do you have planned for your next book?

Funny that you should ask that. Keep reading!

Will we hear from you again?

Definitely! Until next time, here is a little treat to keep you going. Oh, turn to the next page.

THE BOYS ARE BACK!

This time William and Thomas bring even more shenanigans. Follow them as they make their way to the local Comic Fest, host a pool party, sell the neighbour's house (sort of), add a giant TV to their tree fort, and create a birthday to remember. Tidal waves, explosions, falling objects, and angry grannies. What else can happen?

Check out the next page for the

next big adventure of

I TOLD YOU SO!

Chapter 1

The Caps Incident

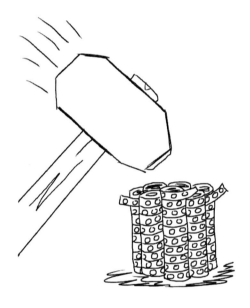

Standing on my driveway I saw William's dad leave for work. William had texted me earlier that morning to tell me to wait until his dad had left. I was to head straight over as soon as I saw him leave. There was no warning as to what was about to go down. I hopped on my bike and pedalled as fast as I could to William's house. I was so excited to find out what was going on that I rode right into his garage with my bike. I skidded to a halt beside his workbench and quickly looked at the plans he had on the board. They looked interesting, as did all of William's plans. William wasn't in the garage yet, so I studied them very carefully. I wasn't quite sure what the first plan was about.

It looked like a picture of William and I and he had a hammer or rubber mallet in his hand. I was apparently taking a picture of him and there appeared to be some type of camera or something on a tri-pod recording us I guess.

The strange part was that there was an object on the floor that William was about to crush with the hammer. It was some type of small roll or a cylinder of some sort. In the background was his dad's pool table, so I knew this was going to take place in the basement. This must have been why he was waiting for his dad to leave.

I began to think of all the various items that the object could be and thought maybe it was a giant marshmallow. However, that idea seemed rather dumb to me, so I began to think of other things. Then the side door to the garage flung open and William came bustling in towards the workbench. William was carrying a small box that he had partially concealed in his hand. I then turned to look at the next plan…

Now it's your turn to draw your own plan for William. Have fun and create what you think will happen next!

Please feel free to send your idea in and share it with the author. Just visit the website for more details at:

www.itchygooneybooks.com

See you next time!

www.itchygooneybooks.com

www.facebook.com/itchygooneybooks/

 @MGunningAuthor

 @markgunningitys

Manufactured by Amazon.ca
Acheson, AB